Katie called after him, "See you tomorrow," but he didn't stop to reply.

At the same moment, Katie's dad appeared. "Who was that you were talking to, Katie?" he asked.

"My friend, Ferguson," said Katie absentmindedly.

"I didn't see anyone down here. Where did he go?" asked her dad.

"Into the long grass," said Katie.

At supper that evening Katie's dad said, "Tomorrow is Saturday and I am going to cut the long grass at the bottom of the garden and clear out those blackberry bushes. There are too many wild creatures living there and eating our vegetables and fruit."

"No dad!" cried Katie. "That is their home."

"Katie, don't worry! They will find a new home somewhere else," said her mother.

"But, Mommy, how would you like to lose your home? The garden has been their home for ever so long. They were here before us. Can't we all live together?" pleaded Katie.

"Darling, you know how much the vegetable garden means to daddy. We can't have the animals eating all the vegetables after all the hard work he has put in growing them."

That night Katie couldn't stop thinking about her friends and the terrible thing that would happen to them tomorrow. She was especially worried about the babies and Mrs. Plover's eggs. She would never see Ferguson again! She was sure that Ferguson would think it all happened because of her.

In the morning Katie got up as soon as it was light and crept down to the basement. There she found a big ball of string and a big piece of cardboard. On the cardboard she wrote: Animal Home. Do Not Touch.

Going to where the long grass started, she tied the string to a tree on one side. Then she stretched the string across the garden and tied it to a tree on the other side. Katie had just finished when her mom and dad came up.

Gathering Katie in her arms her mother said, "Katie we were worried. We didn't know where you were. It's not like you to be down here so early in the morning." Then they saw the fence made of string and read the notice on the cardboard sign.

"Katie your string fence has given me an idea," said her dad. "Instead of cutting the grass and driving the animals away, I will put a fence around my vegetables and build a cage over the fruit and then the animals can stay."

That morning, instead of cutting down the grass and the blackberry bushes, Katie and her dad went to the garden shop and bought wire netting.

In the afternoon, Katie helped her dad build a fence for the vegetable garden and a cage for the fruit garden.

Now in their garden everyone
lives happily together and
Katie sees her friend Ferguson
every day.

About P. Buckley Moss

Born in Staten Island in 1933, P. Buckley Moss (Pat) graduated in 1955 from The Cooper Union, the prestigious New York College for the Arts and the Sciences. The mother of four daughters and two sons, Pat has received numerous honors and awards including a major exhibition of her paintings and etchings in the Tokyo Metropolitan Museum, honorary doctorates and degrees from universities and colleges, and her appointment as a Cultural Laureate of the Commonwealth of Virginia.

Her success is recognized as an example of a triumph over the handicap of dyslexia. Unable to read to any degree of proficiency (she read her first complete novel at age 58), she has used her art from an early age as the means of communicating her love of children and family.

Pat's experience of being dyslexic has made her an ardent advocate for children with special needs. The P. Buckley Moss Society, with its twenty thousand members comprised of collectors of Pat's paintings and prints, and The P. Buckley Moss Foundation for Children's Education are two organizations which, together with Pat and her husband Malcolm, work on behalf of children.

About Malcolm Henderson

Born in England in 1933, Malcolm Henderson came to the United States in 1975 to open an art gallery in Washington, DC. There he met the artist P. Buckley Moss (Pat) and subsequently became both her agent and her husband. Malcolm has four sons and lives with Pat in St. Petersburg, Florida, and Mathews, Virginia.

An exceptionally poor student in school, Malcolm was persistently at the bottom of his class and suffered the ignominy that goes with being unable to learn in a competitive classroom. Thanks to the dedication of one teacher, Hamish Rutherford, who spent endless evenings working with him on Latin prose, the doors to learning were opened.